Lizard People

A Novella

Ryan Rivas

Lizard People
Copyright © 2023 Ryan Rivas
All rights reserved.

No part of this publication may be reproduced,
distributed, or transmitted in any form or by any
means, including photocopying, recording, or other
electronic or mechanical methods, without the prior
written permission of the publisher, except in brief
quotations embodied in critical reviews, citations,
and literary journals for noncommercial uses
permitted by copyright law.

This is a work of fiction. Names, characters,
businesses, places, events, locales, and incidents are
either the products of the author's imagination or
used in a fictitious manner. Any resemblance to
actual persons, living or dead, or actual events is
purely coincidental.

ISBN-13: 979-8-9861105-8-5
Cover art and design by Angelo Maneage
Edited by Maryam Qureshi
Printed in the U.S.A.

For more titles and inquiries, please visit:
www.thirtywestph.com

for Chelsea

Lizard People

Δ

I was sent to the coast for immersion therapy. I'd told my cubemate it was for the humid air, for my lungs, but when I arrived at the resort, the weather was abnormally cold and dry. Only Karen knew the truth. On the day of the trip she'd found me in the copy room with my face pressed to the warm glass, dewlap untucked from my oxford. Karen had always been a discreet coworker. She'd witnessed an incident the month prior and had taken my side for the official report, but she didn't know that I had since been referred to a specialist, hence my trip to the coast. I explained everything, and she seemed to understand. She laughed, though not in a cruel way. "You're a strange one," she said, "but you're pure." The hug was as pleasant as it was unexpected. We had not so much as shaken hands until that moment. "Whatever they're selling you," she said, mid-embrace, "don't buy it." And with that, I left the windowless office in the city for the resort.

Blue skies. Blue ocean. Palms waving hesitantly, like one does to a stranger they've mistaken for a friend. There was a chill in the air but it was nice in the sun, by the pool, and the other poolgoers didn't seem to mind my appearance. Perhaps people were more open-minded on the coast.

Δ

The latest therapist said hypnosis would help me access memories as early as infancy. I lay on his couch in the dark office, eyes closed, overcome with feelings of warmth and serenity. As he counted down from ten, light seemed to flood the room, and when I opened my eyes I was not supine on a therapist's couch but staring at the mobile in my childhood bedroom. Stars and birds and cotton-ball clouds hung from string and spun in slow circles. I'd brought language with me to describe these objects that, at six months old, I could have only absorbed as shapes and colors, sounds and smells. Mother's song drifting down the hallway, crisp and clear. *Blossom of snow, may you bloom and grow.* The smell of bacon in the kitchen. Morning. The morning light, dappled on the ceiling, interrupted by mother's pale face, so young and free of wrinkles, her blue eyes specked with black flakes. She reached into the crib to lift me, her long fingers outstretched and tipped with dark claws.

Δ

I walked the grounds of the resort accompanied by a nurse. My companion and I strolled in full sun along a wide pedestrian path lined with palms. The sand-dusted concrete followed the coastline within earshot of the waves.

"It's cold here," I said.

The nurse nodded. "Supposed to be colder tomorrow."

"I may need to lay out again soon."

"That's fine, but let's keep walking for now."

At some point the path left the resort grounds and passed through a neighborhood of bungalows, low and flat. Staked into the grass of each yard were bright red signs with bold white letters reading NO DESTINY.

"No destiny?" I said.

"No density," the nurse said.

"It says destiny."

"Must be a typo. People can read entire paragraphs of mangled grammar without losing the gist." The nurse chuckled. "The mind sees what it wants to see."

"I see," I said. "But what does it mean?"

"Oh," the nurse said. "It's part of an ongoing anti-development campaign from before the resort was built. The locals don't want more people, more cars, or any more traffic in the neighborhood."

"Invasive species," I said.

"Something like that," the nurse said. We paused where the path curved away from the coast and into town, where the palms gave way to oaks and shade. The nurse crouched down to meet my gaze. "Would you like to keep going?" he asked.

"I think I'd like to go back now."

"Okay," the nurse said. "Can we try it on two legs this time?"

Δ

The therapist said the delusion was imprinted deeper than he'd thought. As usual I lay on the couch while he asked me questions.

Father had obsessed over the lizard people for as long as I could remember. He spent day and night on the computer in the basement. This was part of his work, which he sometimes called his research, and which I always assumed had something to do with the lizard people.

And so it was, at the age of five, when I woke one morning with my arm covered in scales, I knew who I really was.

Mother usually sang to me in the morning. I heard her dulcet tones approaching, crooning that innocent and familiar tune. But when she entered my bedroom that day, I held up the scaled arm and she stifled a scream. Father was already in the basement. Mother's hands slid from her face to her collarbone, fingers resting on the ridge as if inspecting it. She told me to dress quietly and everything would be okay. She wept at every stoplight on the drive to the doctor's office.

The doctor helped calm her. He applied a clear ointment to my arm that smelled like something mother might use to clean the house. I was to apply this twice a day for seven days, the doctor said, and the scales would disappear. Mother wept again outside the doctor's office. The ointment caused my arm to glisten in the sun, bringing out the beauty of the scales in gradients of red, orange, and yellow. I wanted to run my finger across them but I'd been instructed against this impulse. I thought about what might happen if I disobeyed the doctor and refused to apply the ointment, about how my whole body would look covered in scales. Mother collected herself and we got in the car. "Please don't tell your father," she said, and it was then that I understood. She'd been keeping her identity a secret, too.

Mother formed the plan on the ride home. I was to wear long-sleeve shirts during the treatment, despite the warm weather. She said to pretend it was part of a phase, that everyone in my kindergarten class was doing it. But none of this turned out to matter. We rounded the corner onto our street only to find it swarming with black SUVs. Federal agents had stormed the house and taken father.

Δ

On the first full day at the resort I was forced to attend what the therapist called a recovery circle. I was relieved, at least, that I did not have to disguise myself in clothes, though I was surprised that the other participants, all of them middle-aged men, also decided to show up in the nude. Still, I kept an open mind, as this seemed to be the practice in these parts.

The mood was pleasant until the therapist appeared.

"Why are you wearing clothes?" a particularly hirsute man asked the therapist.

"It's customary for humans to be clothed in public," the therapist said.

A different man, this one quite hairless, pointed to the hirsute nude and said, "But *he's* a human."

"I am not!" the hirsute nude said.

"You look like a stark-naked man to me," the hairless nude said.

I soon understood what was happening and spoke up: "He's just in disguise. Surely you understand the need to hide. We've been hiding all our lives, haven't we?"

"I see," said the hairless nude.

I did not comment on the fact that he too appeared to be a naked human being. Apart from mother, I had yet to meet another lizard person, though it appeared as though I was now surrounded by them, albeit in disguise. Some looked sullen, even territorial. But most, myself included, seemed wary, reluctant to engage. I assumed we were all there for the same reason, that the "naked men" around me were also on a path to self-discovery, still concealing their scales out of fear or habit, their nudity a small step toward living in their true skin.

The hairless nude apologized to his hirsute counterpart, who seemed perplexed but pacified by my observation. Apropos of nothing, the therapist declared: "You are all human beings," to which everyone in the recovery circle responded with raucous laughter.

Δ

The government had seized our home, forcing mother and I to move to an apartment while father awaited trial. A few of our new neighbors were friends of my parents' from what mother referred to as "the wild old days." She never explained why father was arrested, only that he'd done nothing wrong.

The ointment made the scales vanish, and yet I could not stop imagining myself covered in them. Despite our similar appearances, I knew I was different from the other boys in the neighborhood. After school we would climb a large oak in a nearby park. The boys would hang from branches and shoot each other with pretend guns. I was content to lay out on a branch in a patch of sunlight. Though it bothered no one, this behavior was especially upsetting to one boy, who one day decided to push me off my perch. I landed on my back, just missing a tree root. Too stunned to cry, deep frantic breaths escaped my mouth like air from a tire. I could not control it, this inward squeal, this outward hiss. It felt strange, unlike me, but soon I realized that this was my true voice. The boy who had pushed me jumped down from the tree and stood over me. He looked horrified at what he'd done. When the boy reached a tentative hand out to help me up, I latched on to the meat between his thumb and forefinger and did not let go.

By age seven I had no friends in the neighborhood, but I understood why. I was not ashamed, which perhaps was thanks to father. Before they'd taken him away, when he was not hard at work in the basement, he was always telling us to be proud of our heritage, extolling the virtues of our people. That's how he always put it: our people, as in, "Our people are natural leaders," and so on. But these reveries always turned bitter, as father inevitably shifted focus to the lizard people. "They threaten to destroy everything our people have worked so hard to build," he'd say. According to father, the lizard people were a cabal of stealthy shapeshifters bent on world domination. They were as powerful and brilliant as they were evil, and so, be I human or lizard person, popular or friendless, I was certainly not short on self-esteem.

In remembering father, which I often did in his absence, I came to understand why mother had kept our shared secret. Surely the truth would have crushed him, and yet, being a child, I was convinced that honesty was the best policy, that father would see we were not evil and love us regardless. But I had no way to reach him. Mother did not visit him, did not speak of him anymore. And yet, I could tell she missed him terribly, that hiding her true self, our true selves, was painful for her. She'd gained a lot of weight. Her hair had lost its shine. Dark circles had taken up permanent residence around her eyes. In this way, her disguise was all the more elaborate.

One morning, over breakfast, I worked up the courage to explain my position. "We shouldn't be afraid of who we are," I said.

Mother smiled and nodded, tears in her eyes. "You're right, honey."

I stared at her longingly while lapping at the bowl below.

"Stop that!" mother screamed, pounding her fist on the kitchen table. "Can you just act normal for once please?"

These mood swings were common. In father's absence, I'd stepped into the role of counterpoint to negativity and self-loathing. "Be proud of your heritage," I said. "We're brilliant and powerful!"

At this she smiled, and her expression softened.

"And we're not evil!"

She broke into laughter. "Of course we're not evil, honey."

She reached her hands across the table and set them on mine. "Your father's trial starts tomorrow," she explained. The trial was set in a different state, and mother would have to spend weeks in a motel. One of her old friends, Judy in 2E, had agreed to watch over me during the ordeal. Her son was the boy who'd pushed me out of the tree. He was a year older but went to the same school. Mother stood, not letting go of my hands. I stood too and she pulled me into an embrace, held me in her arms and cried and cried. Then, like old times, she sang. *Edelweiss, edelweiss, every morning you greet me.* She sang in a whisper, the softness scraped from her voice. At the end of each verse a tender note shined through, as if the melody was about to emerge, and she would sustain it for as long as she could until her voice broke.

$$\Delta$$

Because the morning had gone awry, the afternoon group session was cancelled and we were free to roam the grounds. I chose to stay by the pool, taking my lunch there as well, despite several gentle visits from a nurse, who urged me to take a stroll, to try out the fitness center, to have dinner in the restaurant as opposed to poolside, where many men from the group session also preferred to be. I declined. It was good to be among my people, so to speak. When the sun set and the air grew crisp, I retreated to my room and turned the heat to max.

A light on the phone blinked to indicate a new voicemail. It was Karen from work, sweet Karen, checking in on me. After a few opening pleasantries, her voice became tense. "At first I thought they were sending you to anger management. Then I thought, he doesn't have an angry bone in his body. And then it clicked," she said, pausing in search of the right words. "This is a deprogramming operation." As the message played, I grew more and more confused. Karen proceeded to declare her love for me, in so many words. I did not doubt her sincerity, though I wondered about the suddenness of the declaration. She said she'd been let go from the office and would arrive at the resort tomorrow night. It sounded like she had more to say, but she'd already gone on too long and the machine cut her off.

I replayed Karen's voicemail and sat on the windowsill above the heater to ponder her words. Karen knew my secret and accepted me despite it. She believed therapy was dangerous and feared it would change me. She did not want me to change. She loved me. I listened again and again, moving between phone and sill, until the facts of the matter accumulated and resolved into a conclusion: Karen was a lizard person, too.

I didn't know how to know if I was in love, though I wondered if it mattered. Mate selection was the female's domain. I did know that.

Δ

Judy in 2E reminded me of mother. They wore similar clothes and jewelry, and Judy had an identical cross tattoo on her neck, though mother's was above her left wrist. On the first night of my stay, I couldn't eat a bite of dinner, but no one made an issue of it. Judy and the boy ate in polite silence. Judy put my food in tupperware and said she'd warm it up for me if I got hungry. Later, the boy and I played with pro wrestling action figures in his room.

"My mom says your father is a great man."

"He is," I said. "He didn't do anything wrong."

"She said they trumped up his charges."

I didn't know exactly what this meant, so I said nothing and continued flipping the action figure in front of me, trying to get it to land on its feet.

"Are you sure you're not hungry?" the boy asked. "I can sneak us some ice cream when mom goes to bed."

I thanked him but declined. Perhaps reading too much into his kindness, I used this moment to explain that I'd really prefer to eat crickets.

The boy's face squinched. But then, with more curiosity than judgement, he asked if I was serious.

I told him that I was brilliant and powerful, and that I was supposed to be eating crickets. Mother had forbidden this, of course, and yet I was certain she'd have been too ashamed to mention anything about my eating habits to Judy.

The boy laughed and said I was one strange kid, but that tomorrow we could go find some crickets.

The next day at dismissal we met behind the school. The boy had filled a brown paper bag with live crickets. "I collected them during P.E." he said.

"You're a good friend," I said.

As I reached for the bag, he pulled it closer to his chest. "Don't you think I should feed them to you?"

"I'm not a pet!" I said.

"I guess you're right," my new friend said, looking at his shoes before looking up again and saying, "But then, shouldn't you, like, hunt them?"

It was a fair compromise for his good deed, and we got along like this for a week or so, until one day when we decided to play by the oak tree in the park. I was lying on my favorite branch and my friend was digging around in the dirt when a group of older boys approached.

"Come down from there," they called. "We heard you have a trick to show us."

My friend looked nervous, but he nodded for me to obey. I climbed down and the boys closed in on us. My friend pulled a worm from his shirt pocket. "Watch this!" he said. He turned to me. "Open wide."

I opened my mouth to receive the worm with pleasure, eyes trained on the boys encircling us, who erupted in cries of *eeeew* and *gross*. One boy vomited on his own shoes and the crowd erupted again. Though one boy remained silent throughout, glowering, arms crossed over his chest. As the other boys collected themselves, he finally spoke: "You're a fucking freak!"

"I know!" my friend said. "It's freaky, right?"

"You're a freak too!" the boy said, uncrossing his arms. "What the hell is wrong with you?"

I stayed still but kept an eye trained on the boy. I understood exactly what was happening. The boy puffed out his chest and took a step toward my friend. That's when I pounced.

On the one hand, perhaps my friend did think of me as a pet. On the other, he was the only one who gave me what I craved.

Δ

The therapist apologized for the previous day. He explained that the group session had been intended to acclimate his patients to the concept of immersion therapy before beginning the actual process. It had failed spectacularly, he said, though his tone was upbeat.

"It was nice to be among my people," I said.

The therapist leaned back and crossed his legs. We were in his hotel room, in a set of plush chairs by a window overlooking the ocean. Piles of newspaper and magazine clippings were scattered on the table between us.

"Do you remember why you're here?" he asked.

"To embrace my true self," I said. "To stop hiding."

"Very good," he said. "And who are you?"

I stated my name, place of birth, the names of my immediate family and all the other biographical information in the long mantra the therapist had prescribed, but I stopped short of the last part.

The therapist moved nothing but his lips. "And what species are you?"

"I can't say what you want me to say."

"Okay then," the therapist said. "What do you want to say?"

"There is no known scientific classification. The closest equivalent is likely Animalia chordata reptilia squamata iguania iguanidae iguana i. iguana," I said earnestly.

The therapist uncrossed his legs and leaned forward, resting his elbows on the table and folding his hands. "You are not here to more fully become a lizard," he said. "You are here to be freed of this very delusion."

"If you say so," I said, assessing the angle at which the therapist leaned, somewhere between threatening and playful.

"Let's step back a moment. Do you remember why you began seeing me in the first place?"

"As a condition of my employer," I answered, watching his hands closely. They were pale and manicured, smooth and still.

"That's correct. Your employer required it. Do you remember why?"

"Accosting a coworker."

"Good. And why did you accost this coworker?"

"He cornered me in the breakroom. No one else was around. He wanted to destroy my kind, he said. He raised his fists, so I protected myself."

"And why did he want to, as you say, 'destroy your kind'? What do you think he meant by 'your kind'?"

"Lizard people, of course."

"But if you were in hiding, as we've discussed in past sessions, how did he know you were a lizard person?"

"Some people can tell, like father. He knew about several lizard people, certain celebrities, public officials in positions of power, hiding in plain sight."

"But as you yourself claim, your father never suspected his own family of being lizards."

"Not lizards. Lizard *people*. Mother and I were very good at hiding. And sometimes, when you're close to someone, it's difficult to see the obvious."

"A very pertinent observation. Very true. Especially with regard to family, it's often difficult to see what's right in front of us. Perhaps this is why you could not foresee what would happen to your mother?"

I hissed. It was instinct. My dewlap pulsed against my shirt collar. I had dressed out of respect for the therapist's wishes, and now he was making me regret it. I stood, preparing to run away.

"I think that's enough for today," he said, slowly unfolding his hands, palms up, and sinking back into the chair. "We'll resume tomorrow morning, same time."

I darted from the room, undoing the top three buttons of my oxford for relief. I did not like to think about mother's demise. She never fully embraced who she was. She couldn't live with herself. The shame drove her to do the unthinkable.

Δ

Father was sentenced to life in prison and mother moved us to a mobile home park on the outskirts of a desert city. I had so many questions about father, about our new home, about everything. Why had mother forced me to grow out my hair while she'd cut hers short and dyed it brown? Why had she stopped wearing jewelry and makeup? Why had she modified her cross tattoo to look like a kite?

She warned me never to speak about the past again or I would regret it, and so I was frightened into obedience. Though the trial had lasted only a month, it had changed her, made her stricter, colder. It was like living with a stranger. She didn't sing to me anymore. Silence was now the norm in the household.

By the time I started middle school, mother had lost double the weight she'd gained before father's trial, and I'd retreated deep into myself. This was when I began seeing the first of many therapists. I did not ask why, nor did I express the opinion that mother might also benefit from such care. She at least looked the part of mother when dropping me off three days a week, dressed in her diner uniform, before heading to her usual double-shift.

Though I never understood why I was in therapy, the therapists were kind conversationalists who filled the verbal void at home. My first was particularly paternal. He asked what I'd learned in school and even helped with homework. After each session, I was trusted to walk myself home. A few blocks from the office park was the riverwalk, and I followed its dusty path two miles out of the city, homeward. On these walks I was free to be me, to sprint through the reeds at the river's edge, to scuttle up and down the highway underpasses, to catch bugs, to hide under rocks, to swim.

I had all the time in the word to explore the natural surroundings, as mother worked until long after I was asleep. She didn't work Sundays, which she spent laying out in a lawn chair, sunrise to sunset, tanning. I'd come home from wandering to find her red as an apple, and on days when there was no therapy, I'd return from school to find her sitting on the couch peeling long translucent strips of skin from her arms and legs. This seemed to bring her peace. I would sit beside her and watch television for a few hours before she left for her shift. This was our routine, our silent bonding.

Δ

I had room service bring a platter of lettuce in preparation for Karen's arrival. While I was familiar with the love of family, I had not yet found a suitable mate. I'd never given it much thought, to be honest, but when Karen appeared in the doorway, I was reassured by her loose, botanical-print dress that instinct would guide me. I invited her to join me at the table by the window.

"Oh," she said, eyeing the lettuce. "What do you have in store for us?"

"I thought we might get hungry," I said. "I don't like eating in the restaurant."

"This is much more intimate."

I agreed, and we talked for a long time, bypassing the water-cooler conversations of our previous interactions for the serious dialogue of two misunderstood souls connecting at last.

Karen confessed that she often hid her true self from others, and I realized we were even more alike than she knew. She never explicitly mentioned family, but I could tell from her expression that she'd borne the pain of keeping secrets from loved ones, had lived in fear of their prejudice and scorn. Karen was never comfortable around our coworkers, she admitted, especially my assailant. She regretted that I'd been, as she put it, "sentenced to the headshrinkers" after the incident. I reassured her that all was well, that I'd been through more therapists than anyone could imagine. Not one of them understood me or accepted me. This one was no different, and I would endure.

"That's good," Karen said. "Still, our people have to look out for each other, you know?"

An uncanny scent filled the room. I breathed it in, and my head felt hollow even as it seemed to swell.

"Deprogrammers can be sneaky," Karen said. "Are you managing to resist their lies?"

"I suppose you could put it that way." As my head shrank back down to size, a tingling sensation took over, a numbness of the skull I'd once experienced after drinking too much champagne. "Today was tough, though," I said. "Mother came up."

"It's a shame what the feds put her through."

I glanced down at the clatter of my claws gripping the edge of the table. I had not instructed them to do so, focused as I was on suppressing a hiss amid the shock of this revelation. "You knew mother?" I managed to say.

"Don't look so surprised. I know all about your family. Only from what I've read, of course. What else do you think attracted me to you?"

So she'd known all along how alike we were. Perhaps years of therapy did damage me, I thought, otherwise I'd have recognized her as a soulmate much sooner. The scent was stronger now. It seemed to course through my blood. My whole body tingled.

"I know a lot more about your father, though," Karen said. "He was a great man."

"Yes, he was," I said, pleased to hear her positive opinion of father despite his views on our kind. She really did understand. It must have been why she'd chosen me.

"They treated him so poorly," Karen said. "At least he got to pass on his good genes."

"He was framed," I said.

"Oh yeah?" she said.

"Framed by lizard people."

"Of course he was!" she said through her laughter. "Now *those* bastards are sneaky!"

"We're not all evil, though," I said, as if she didn't already know.

"Is that so?" she said.

"Do I look evil to you?"

Karen stood and slid the dress off her shoulders. She turned slowly, revealing a cross tattoo on her lower back that looked like mother's before she'd turned it into a kite. I reached my hand across the table to trace the tattoo and Karen shivered.

"Don't be shy," she said. "Let's see what you're hiding under there."

My head bobbed with excitement. After that unpleasant session with the therapist I'd been aching to strip down to my skin, but I'd kept my clothes on, the same oxford and khakis I wore each day to work, to create a kind of continuity for Karen, a smooth transition before revealing my true self.

I rose from the chair. Karen continued to spin in slow circles. I could not help but think of the mobile from childhood, though I understood that what was before me was something entirely different. She spun her way to the edge of the bed, where she sat, calling me over with a wave.

I undressed where I stood and followed her to the bed, crouching down so we were face to face. I rested my claws on her knees. Karen leaned in and nuzzled my dewlap. She placed slow kisses over every inch of my jowls. She caressed my face, ran her hand along my dorsal crest. By now my head was bobbing at a steady rhythm. Karen withdrew and looked into my eyes. She placed her hand atop my bobbing head and kept it there, gently guiding me down. Then, she began to moan.

Δ

My high school years brought even more freedom, but school itself was confining. People paid more attention to me despite my desire to be overlooked. I was a quiet student with no friends, sitting alone at lunch, darting to and from classes to avoid hallway confrontations. I was called many names, but never anything lizard-related. There was a clique of boys who preferred variations on "evil," as in "evil sonofabitch" and "evil motherfucker." Another clique never said a word, rather they would lock eyes with me and strike out with a fierce chopping motion, sometimes at a distance, sometimes up close, stopping within inches of my face. I sensed more of my kind existed among the student body, but imagined they were too afraid of reprisal to seek camaraderie. Yet another clique would choose certain days to reign terror on this timid species of student. I'd spend those days locked in a stall in the girls' bathroom, sitting atop the tank, feet on the toilet seat, reading a novel or studying for a test. Soon I spent every lunch period this way, hiding from those who would like to see me bloody. By then I'd become a vegetarian and ate mostly lettuce, which was another reason to hide during lunch, to avoid endless harassment for my diet. My eating habits also suited me at home, where the oven had gone unused since we moved in.

The timid students eventually formed a clique of their own, but they avoided my gaze as if it was lethal. Even from afar, as I spotted the frail herd in the halls among the crush of students, my meager waves went ignored. I once tried to join them at a lunch table, only to be told my kind wasn't welcome. I should have known, given past experience, that I was not built for humanoid friendship. The rejection did not hurt. Though lizard people are coldblooded only in the literal sense, I was content in my solitude. Alone, not lonely. As I had come to understand, it was not so much self-esteem that helped me through my schooling years, rather, I simply did not feel the need for emotional connection. At least when it came to those outside my immediate family.

Like any curious and sad teenager in my situation would do, I tried to contact father. Though mother's attention was scant, I kept my project hidden, for any mention of father would send her into hysterics.

It was not difficult to find him. I called the prison but was told I could not visit or even speak to father. He was being held indefinitely in solitary confinement. Given the setback, I researched father's trial and conviction. My therapist at the time referred to this as a "positive expression of rebellion," as he thought mother's rule against contacting father was repressive.

Father had always been a peripheral subject in therapy, probably because my memories of him were few and happy, and past therapists had treated his absence as a kind of death. Perhaps they too were unaware of his alleged criminality. This particular therapist, however, encouraged me to discover the truth.

I was shocked by what I found. Father had been imprisoned for a long list of crimes including extortion, kidnapping, and murder. He'd not been charged with committing the crimes himself, rather, he was considered responsible for influencing these various offenses. He allegedly provided coded instructions via his radio show, which at least shed some light on what he'd been up to in the basement all those years. I was learning so much about father, the therapist considered this to be a potential break-through moment.

To read about father in the mainstream newspapers, you'd think he was an evil mastermind. This was, I discovered via several other sources, no coincidence. For every damning headline there were dozens of posts and threads pointing to evidence that father had been framed by lizard people. Though recordings of father's show had been removed from the internet by court order, there was no shortage of broadcasts and websites dedicated to tracking a nefarious cabal of lizard people who pulled the strings of power. I listened and learned. Apparently, accusing one's enemy of what one is guilty of was a known modus operandi of the lizard people, or I should say, this particular group of lizard people, as not all lizard people are alike. I had no doubt my father was framed, and likely by lizard people, but I took issue with how these whistleblowers painted an entire species with such a broad brush.

And there I was again, trapped between two worlds. I must admit that while these reports vindicated father and brought me relief, they also rekindled painful memories of being misjudged as evil simply because of who I was. How could I ever shake the hands of my father's defenders without concealing a part of myself? There would be no convincing them of my innocence.

I explained all of this to the therapist, the words pouring out of me. When I finished, a long silence lapsed while I awaited his analysis. Never before had I shared so much in a session, and never before had a therapist's guidance seemed so crucial. How could I forget the gold watch around his thick hairy wrist, the deafening clicks of its second hand?

At last, he responded, all the gentleness of past sessions drained from his voice. "I'm afraid you are in deep, deep denial," he said. He continued speaking for several minutes, refuting every detail of my story. He rejected not only father's innocence, but the very existence of his persecutors. "These lizard people are a delusion," he said. "A delusion of very troubling origins."

That was when I explained to him, quite calmly, that lizard people were not a monolith, that there were good ones and bad ones, just like any other species, and that I knew this because I myself was a lizard person.

Despite his stern tone, the therapist's expression had remained neutral until this point, when a frown formed that caused the whole lower half of his face to sag. His eyes lost their focus, looking not at but through me, filled with what I knew to be fear.

"This is above my paygrade," he said.

And with that, I was sent to a specialist.

Δ

When I woke the next morning, Karen was gone. Perhaps she was already gravid and had gone off to perform some evolutionary duty. Though I was a bit embarrassed by my ignorance, I felt quite relaxed nonetheless. I picked at the lettuce on the table, which had remained untouched since the night before, thinking about fatherhood.

When I returned to the therapist's room later that morning, he was not alone. Two figures sat at the table by the window. The curtain was closed, making it difficult to distinguish their features in the dim light.

The therapist greeted me warmly but stayed in the threshold. "Let me take this moment to prepare you," he said. "Today's session will be more intense than the last."

He moved aside, inviting me into the room. The figures had not turned toward the door, had not moved at all, and I soon realized it was because they were dummies, the kind seen in department stores. One wore a blonde wig and a blue turtleneck sweater. The other was left bald and wore a white undershirt. There was an empty chair beside each of them, presumably reserved for me and the therapist. The table was cleared of the news clippings from the day before, which I had not paid any attention to at the time. They'd been moved to the foot of the bed, and this time I took a moment to examine them. Looking down at what the therapist had laid out, I was horrified to discover photos of father, articles about the trial, the unsuccessful appeals, and father's untimely end. Above the bed hung a curtain I had not seen in a long time. Though I was never allowed into father's basement office, anyone walking by our home could see it draped over the high window: white fabric with a black cross inside a circle, an extra bar bent inward, encroaching on the otherwise symmetrical design. I'd always thought of it as a curtain, actually. It had never seemed like a flag until I saw it there hanging flaglike above the bed.

"We're going to do some role-playing today," the therapist said. "Let's have a seat, shall we?"

I faltered toward the table and sat next to the blonde dummy.

"Quite an interesting choice," the therapist said, walking over to join me.

"What could you possibly mean by that?"

"Apologies," the therapist said. "I'm getting ahead of myself." He sat in the adjacent chair, clutching a small stack of white paper which he set on his lap. "This dummy," he said, pointing to the blonde, "represents your mother. And this one," pointing beside him, "represents your father. What you've done just now, consciously or, more likely, unconsciously, is chosen your mother."

"I haven't chosen a thing!" I said, too confused to be nervous. "What does any of this have to do with me?"

"I've created a script with several short scenes," he said, patting the paper on his lap. "Each scene is based on a memory you've described in our sessions. Of course, our memories are imperfect and incomplete. These scenes fill certain informational gaps which, due to your condition, you have been unable to process. We will rehearse these scenes daily until we've internalized them, much like your mantra."

Perspiration dotted the therapist's hairline and upper lip. It occurred to me that he'd adjusted the temperature so I would be comfortable, which made me warm to him a bit.

"Now then," he said. "Let's continue the difficult work of letting go of this deep-seated delusion."

Δ

One night during my junior year, mother called in sick to work for the first time ever. As I did homework at the kitchen table, she popped a bottle of champagne. "Take a break," she said. "Let's celebrate. It's homecoming!"

I informed her that homecoming was not for another few weeks, a bit of useless knowledge as far as I was concerned, though no less true.

"It's homecoming somewhere," she said. She set two pebbled tumblers from the diner on the table and poured the fizzy liquid into them.

We sat on the couch and watched television. I sipped the champagne like a human, but its tartness caused my tongue to shoot out in all directions. Mother laughed and said I didn't have to drink it if I didn't like it.

I drank it nonetheless, to please her, because it seemed so few things brought her pleasure, and I was glad that my presence was one of those things. It was true, we rarely spoke, but we didn't need to, and mother did speak up when it mattered.

At the time, I was going through specialists as if they were tissues. The sessions would start out fine, then I would describe how father was framed and we'd hit an impasse.

No therapist would believe me. They latched on to the word "frame." It was as if they were all operating out of the same textbook. They wanted to talk about "re-framing my subject position." And they all wanted to give me pills, which I was not yet old enough to decline, but mother acted in my best interest and rejected the medication. "He's not schizo!" she'd scream each time, as a way of saying, in her own way, that we'd be seeking the services of a different mental health professional. In these vital moments, she had not lost her protective instinct.

The night on the couch with the champagne was a good one, and I knew to savor it as such. Eventually we retired to our rooms. Too tired for homework or reading, I fell into a pleasant sleep and woke with the remnants of strange dreams, my computer dinging with a news alert. Father had been found dead in his cell. I clicked the alert box to read the full article. It had happened days ago but was just now being reported. Father had apparently bashed his head against the floor until he passed out, then bled out.

And so my high school years came and went. I enrolled in community college, worked temp jobs for various offices, and stopped going to therapy. I accepted the fact that I would not be accepted for who I am, and life went on.

How did mother feel about father's death? I never discussed it with her. I might have done so, had I known she would do what she did.

"I'm sorry I became distant," she'd written. "My love for you never changed. It's just that I was afraid to be your mom again. I was broken, and you were fragile. You know that, right? After all that happened, I was scared to death I'd break you, too." This rather vague note was all that remained of her. She never got over living in hiding. But we're not here to talk about that, are we?

Δ

When I left the therapist's room the hirsute man was waiting in the hall, dressed for his appointment in a touristy disguise.

"Tough session?" he asked.

I supposed he could read the look on my face. The role-playing had been exhausting and confusing. The therapist had invented stories to fill the so-called gaps in my past, but his scripts were more like nightmares than memories, full of black eyes and broken plates. The therapist would have me believe my childhood home was a pigsty. At one point, he placed the father-dummy's hands around the mother-dummy's neck and made me act out a script with my wrist in a splint.

The hirsute man removed a glass jar from his cargo shorts. Crickets hopped about inside it. He removed the lid and thrust the jar in my direction. "Here," he said. "Have one on me."

I did, and I thanked him.

The therapist emerged from the room and addressed the hirsute man, who stuffed the jar back in his pocket.

"I'm sorry to keep you waiting," the therapist said. "As you can see, the last session ran late and now we've reached the lunch hour. We'll meet back here at one."

The hirsute man nodded. It was embarrassing how he cowered in the therapist's presence.

The therapist closed the door behind him and nodded at me. Something had changed between us. I'd never felt oppressed by him until today, and I began to think Karen was right about his manipulative powers.

"I'll see you gentlemen later." The therapist continued down the hall, clutching a leather binder I'd never seen before, the binder bulging with loose paper. "There's a seafood special in the restaurant today," he said over his shoulder. When the therapist turned the corner at the elevators, the hirsute man retrieved the jar and held it out in offering again.

"Here, have another," he said.

I declined this time, a bit sad that I'd lost the taste for them.

"Suit yourself," the hirsute man said. He tilted his head back and placed the jar's mouth against his own, tapping the base with his free hand. One by one the crickets hopped in, down the hatch. When he finished, he asked if my session had really been that bad.

I needn't do anything but continue looking at him to communicate my reply.

"There are more groups than ours," he said. "They're bringing us all together for some kind of presentation tomorrow. At least it beats this one-on-one stuff, right?"

I feigned a smile, which was unlike me. My thoughts were unusually scattered. The hallway was too dim. I needed light and heat. "Right," I said. "Why don't we go out to the pool and get some sun?"

The hirsute man returned the smile, and together we walked down the hall, the footfall of my brogues muffled compared to my new friend's smacking flip-flops.

We did not make it to the pool. When the elevator doors opened on the lobby, I saw Karen gesturing wildly at the front desk. As I approached, I could hear her saying, "I walked right in here last night with no problem! There wasn't even anyone sitting here!"

"That shouldn't have happened, ma'am," the man behind the desk said. "I just need you to register as a visitor." He slid a clipboard across the desk. Beside the clipboard sat a brown paper bag with a steaming bowl of pasta illustrated on its side.

"I'm not giving you my name," Karen said. "This is America and I have a right to privacy!"

She was so worked up it took her a moment to realize I'd arrived at her side. "You came back," I said.

Karen startled, turned toward me and laughed. "You didn't think I left you, did you?" she said. Her face was glowing. She grabbed the brown bag from the desk and held it up. "I got us lunch," she said.

I was a bit confused by the choice of meal, but I was happy to see Karen. It took me a moment to realize my face hurt, my smile having transformed from fake to genuine at the sight of her.

The man behind the desk stood. "She won't sign in," he said, addressing someone behind us. It was the therapist, a cloth napkin tucked into his oxford. He was carrying the binder.

"Is this him?" Karen asked. Before I could reply she turned to address the therapist. "You!" she said. "You're the one fucking with his head, huh?"

I was alarmed but glad that Karen was defending me.

"You're filling him with lies!" she continued. "You're trying to make him hate himself!"

The therapist remained calm while eyeing the man behind the desk. "On the contrary," he said, looking at Karen now as if she was his patient. "I'm helping him embrace who he is."

"Oh yeah, and who is that?"

"A human being."

"What a crock of shit!" Karen smacked the leather binder out of his hands. "You're vermin!"

As the man behind the desk hustled around to the other side, speaking into his wrist the whole time, Karen treaded backward toward the automatic doors.

"And who, may I ask, are you?" said the therapist.

"Five words," Karen said. "I have nothing to say."

The man behind the desk had summoned a man just like him, smartly dressed in tie and slacks. They stood on either side of Karen with their arms out, creating a kind of path as they shepherded her out the door.

Karen never took her eyes off me. "Stay strong," she said. "We're getting you out of here."

The scene was too shocking to question what she meant by "we." The therapist's papers were scattered across the lobby floor. Once Karen was out of sight, the hirsute man ran up to help collect them, along with a few others who'd been gawking on the peripheries. I bent down beside my hirsute friend. The lobby was cold and the tile floor even colder. I gathered a few errant pages and, without really thinking about it, folded them in half and stuffed them in the hirsute man's cargo pocket. He felt the tug and glanced over. I held a finger to my lips, and he frowned.

Δ

Alone, I sat on the windowsill for a long time, gazing back and forth between the papers and the phone, hoping Karen would call at any minute. I'd hardly noticed the sunset. The room was covered in darkness but for the tiny red light on the phone. I moved to the bed and played her message over and over.

This discomfort I felt, this confusion – was it love? Given the extenuating circumstances of my adolescence, the subject was never broached. Father's name being verboten, I did not ask mother how they met or why she picked him. Had she always been aware of his views on our kind? Had her parents disapproved of *his* kind? All I knew was that love must be complicated, and the thought that this suffering was normal made me feel a little bit better.

I pondered what Karen had said about getting me out and regretted not having the chance to tell her the whole story. While the therapy was mandated, and in that sense, as Karen suggested, I was somewhat trapped, the term of my so-called treatment was not indefinite. If only Karen knew this resort excursion was optional, a way to expedite my sentence. As far as I knew, I was free to leave whenever. If only I could talk to her and put her at ease. It pained me to be causing her pain.

Perhaps I'd been lying there in the darkness too long, because Karen's last words lingered and I began to question whether or not I needed rescuing. If I could leave the resort, why had I never thought about it? Did the therapist have some kind of psychological hold on me? Could he have done something nefarious while I was under hypnosis? Those papers may have contained the answers, but I couldn't bring myself to read them. I turned on the bedside lamp and dismissed my thoughts as paranoid. I didn't need to read those papers because I already knew who I was. I was happy with who I was. I'd met someone who loved me for who I was. Those papers wouldn't tell me anything I didn't already know.

It occurred to me that I had not eaten since the day Karen left her message, so I left my room and sat in the restaurant for the first time, where I was the only patron. I ordered champagne in hopes that I might feel the same way I'd felt with Karen the night before. The waitress brought me a whole bottle. Despite her kindness, there was something off about her. Her wrinkled uniform smelled like cigarette smoke, which seemed unprofessional. I'd barely sipped the champagne when she returned to the table with a plate of shrimp, though I'd been expecting greens. "These are on special," she said. She set the plate down in front of me and kept her hand on it for an unusual amount of time. "But the chef tells me you can order them whenever." I followed her gaze down and saw the tattoo on her exposed wrist. Like mother's. Like Karen's. When I looked up, she winked and let go of the plate. "Karen says hi," she said.

I never saw that woman again. And for the record, I'd see Karen once more, though only from afar.

Δ

The lobby was packed with people, not one of them familiar. It seemed as if every guest at the resort was present, which turned out to be the case. The man behind the desk called for everyone to file into the ballroom. Standing on tiptoes, I looked above a sea of heads toward a hallway off the lobby that led to three sets of double doors. Slowly but surely the crowd shuffled that way, and I could see nurses stationed at each door holding clipboards and handing cards to attendees. When it was my turn to enter, a nurse pressed a card into my hand. "That's your table number," she said. "Hang on to it and go find your group."

The inside of the ballroom was cavernous, the ceiling scaffolded with sound and lighting rigs. At the front of the room was a high stage topped with a mahogany podium, and behind that a massive projection screen. I meandered through offset rows of round tables, on which pads and pens were scattered around tall floral centerpieces. Nurses had spread out among the tables, helping people find their seats by pointing to the numbered cards poking out of the centerpieces. I held my card out to one of them and they pointed me toward the back of the ballroom.

I was relieved to see the hirsute man, the hairless man beside him, and all the others from that first failed group session, sitting at my assigned table. Naturally we were naked, as were the men at some of the other tables. At one nearby table, in addition to being nude, all the men were covered in tattoos. There were also lots of people wearing clothes, button downs and dresses, men and women, the first women I'd seen besides resort employees, and of course Karen. While the clothed people were not mixed with the nudes, I could see some clothed people with no apparent marks mixed with people who were both clothed and tattooed, like the man one table over, whose adam's apple was covered by a startling skull that rattled above his shirt collar as he spoke.

"These are all patients?" I asked the hairless man.

"Looks that way," he said.

My hirsute friend picked up a pen from the center of the table and examined the text on its side. "He had me on this one a while back," he said.

The hairless man looked to his neighbor. "That stuff made me nauseous," he said. "He switched me to something else."

They were talking about medications, I inferred. Medication had been the final straw in my previous experiences with therapy, a fate I avoided thanks to mother. And yet, if I was grouped with these men because the therapist thought us similar, there was a chance he might resort to pills. This worried me quite a bit, though I had no time to fret, as the feedback squealing from the PA system signaled the first speaker.

The therapist fiddled with the microphone from behind the podium. He looked over his shoulder at the blank projection screen and shrugged. "I'm sure we'll get that up and running soon," he said to someone in the wings. "Welcome," he said, addressing everyone else, and that was all he was able to say before the disruption. Another voice cried out, unamplified but nonetheless resounding. It was a woman's voice, and though I was seated too far away to decipher the exact words, I knew it was Karen's.

Her message, whatever it was, was drowned out by the collective gasp of the audience as Karen rushed the stage and pushed the therapist aside to commandeer the podium. The blank screen behind her switched to an image of the curtain, rather, the flag father kept in the basement window, the one the therapist had used as some kind of prop in his role-playing game. I had no idea what any of it meant, and for a brief moment I thought this ruse might have been planned, part of my therapy.

Karen yanked the microphone from its stand. I wished I'd been sitting closer. From this distance, under the stage lights, her face was a white glare. "I've got one message for you twisted fucks," she said. "Let... my... people... go!"

Then, quite dramatically, more flags unfurled all around us, draped from the lighting rigs above. Karen slammed the microphone to the ground and the screech that erupted from the speakers was deafening. People covered their ears, some booed and hissed, others scuttled for the exits, only to be met by a cadre of nurses storming into the ballroom, perhaps doubling as security guards. However, as these nurses did not head for the stage to apprehend Karen, it seemed they were up to something else. They weaved through the tables, arms raised high, each of them clutching some kind of object with a little blue light on the end. The nurses who'd been keeping watch between tables looked around frantically. One of them yelled, "Tazers!" and they began to scatter. But for the nurses closer to the stage, it was too late. The intruders made contact and down they went.

It became clear to me, and soon to others, that these incoming nurses were deranged. The gentleman with the neck tattoo was the first to act. As one intruder chased a nurse past his table, he shot up from his seat and smashed a centerpiece into the intruder's face. This seemed to set off the entire table of nude tattooed men. Chairs toppled back as the men sprang forward to give chase. The air filled with pens, as many in the audience, armed with nothing else, flung them viciously at the intruders. More nurses went down under the shock of tazers, but many more in the audience began to fight back, jumping onto the backs of the intruders and sinking their teeth in wherever they could. The man with the neck tattoo had chased three more intruders into the arms of his tablemates, who held them in full nelsons as the tattooed man delivered a pummeling with mechanical precision. One, two, three, up and down the line. "Stop!" the intruders pleaded between blows. "You don't understand!" they blathered from bloody mouths. "We're trying to free you!" My chest constricted with each strike. The tattooed man's fist was covered in blood. My whole body had gone stiff and I was fixed to the chair, unable to move anything but my eyes.

I looked to the stage and Karen was gone. The therapist lay supine beside the podium, gripping his shin. I was not the only one to see the duo of deranged nurses scrambling across the proscenium to reach him, for a giant specimen of a man had jumped atop a nearby table. A screaming eagle inked across his broad back, he unfurled his impressive wingspan and gave voice to the eagle, a battle cry that brought nearly all the chaos to a halt. The man then leaped from table to table on his way to the stage, pens swarming all around him, until his feet hit the last table and he took flight. The two deranged nurses had already dropped their tazers and lifted their hands in surrender, but it was too late to save them from the clutches of the man's massive biceps.

When all the lunatics appeared to be subdued and the numbers were to their advantage, the actual nurses began herding people out of the ballroom. I was astonished to see all the men at my table sitting there, calm and quiet, expressions blank, as if nothing had happened. Sedated. They had no idea what Karen had tried to do for me, for all of us, and I knew it was because of the drugs. For the first time in a long time, I feared for my future.

Δ

—and given the demographics that have rendered Whiteness normative are no longer operative, the time has come to reexamine a pathology long acknowledged by professionals but obstructed from official diagnosis by centuries of national hegemony. Building on the work of Sullaway and Dunbar (see: Sullaway and Dunbar, appendix iii), whose ground-breaking correlations between prejudice and mental illness have set the stage for a broad reexamination of professional terminology, there has been renewed interest in clinical studies related to the pathology of Whiteness. Indeed, there is much ground to cover and myriad nuances to explore. This paper seeks to revise two specific diagnoses.

The authors have identified a sizable cohort of patients who exhibit characteristics indicative of Dissociative Fugue and Psychogenic Amnesia (see: appendix vi). While a broad range of traumas are associated with these diagnoses, the authors have established that this cohort's dissociative symptoms stem from a singular, causal origin: a confrontation with one's own whiteness. Early studies suggest the primary catalyst for this distinct type of dissociation is rooted in feelings of guilt and overwhelming responsibility for prejudice (be it mild or extreme, personal or systemic, active participation or passive complicity), resulting in a spectrum of responses from denial to delusion. Symptoms include verbal denial, memory loss, and, in the most extreme cases, identity reinvention.

The authors argue these symptoms require special consideration separate from their existing diagnoses under current categories. Such dissociative symptoms should be outgrowths of the pending category of Whiteness. The authors suggest the sub-categorical term Dissociative Whiteness to clearly differentiate between varieties of denial associated with other conditions. As such, existing treatments for recognized dissociative disorders, while instructive, are not sufficient.

The challenge of treatment lies in patients' denial of the underlying pathology, which itself is characterized by symptoms of denial, creating a compound pathology akin to what some cross-disciplinary scholars have termed "epistemologies of ignorance" (see: Mills, appendix iii). The authors report difficulty establishing a baseline from which patients have deviated, and to which they may safely return to begin addressing core, underlying identity issues. Patients who cannot, or refuse to, understand the underlying pathology prove less responsive to treatment. Based on extensive research, interviews, controlled experiments, and various therapeutic methods, the authors have identified three types of denial related to Dissociative Whiteness, with responses to treatment varying based on each patient's understanding of their core pathological identity:

(1) Enlightened Denial. Memory loss tends to be temporary and brief. Patients exhibit firm, if uneasy, understanding of core identity. Condition is often triggered by "ambush" (see: Yancy, appendix iii). Traditional talk therapy sufficient for treatment.

(2) Compound Denial. Sustained memory loss. Fugue state is common and prolonged. Condition is often triggered by an unconscious incident of prejudice made conscious, usually through confrontation. Patients exhibit little to no understanding of core identity. Intense treatment beyond traditional CBT required.

(3) Delusional Denial. Memory loss, alteration, invention, and replacement. Complete identity reinvention. Condition appears to correlate with exposure to extremist identity groups. Additional symptoms resemble monomaniacal zoanthropy with elements of clinical lycanthropy. Experimental treatments in progress (see: appendix xii).

Over the course of several years, the authors have compiled hundreds of case studies, though many treatments remain ongoing, particularly in acute—

Δ

The therapist's papers were riddled with jargon-filled nonsense. Granted it was only an excerpt, I read it three times and still extracted no meaning. Of course, I was exhausted from the madness of the ballroom and even more confused about Karen than before, so I retreated to a poolside lounge chair and promptly fell asleep. I dozed in and out, through lunch and dinner, vaguely aware of the shapes moving around me, the palms overhead, before returning to blissful nothingness. I slept so long that by the time I opened my eyes it was well past midnight and bitter cold. No one was around. I put on my robe for warmth and walked out to where the palm-lined path met the sand.

I admired the moonlit beach, the white sand practically glowing. A strong wind blew ripples over the water and rustled the palms overhead, reminding me of mother's song, and I began to drift into that familiar daydream, the whole family together again, picnicking in a meadow, father in the shade of an umbrella while mother and I lay in the sun, no longer in disguise, all of us happy.

Somewhere above, there was a sound like a piece of celery snapping in half, and right before my eyes a lizard fell to the sand, inert at my feet. I dropped to all fours and lowered myself to the ground to get a closer look at this poor, beautiful creature that had not evolved to withstand the frigid air. It lay on its back, body in rigor.

The long gust continued blowing and I watched another one fall in my periphery. It barely made a sound as it hit the sand, unmoving. Soon they were dropping all around me as the wind picked up and emptied the palms.

But I did not fret, for I knew this was not the end. I removed my robe before returning my belly to the cold path. I wanted them to recognize me as one of their own. I waited, so ecstatic I could not sleep, would not shut my eyes. All I could do was bob my head until the sky turned rosy and the sun peeked over the horizon.

A few early morning joggers and dogwalkers came upon the scene. Some stopped several yards from me, daunted perhaps by the cluttered path, and turned around. But most kept a wide berth and took a detour through the sand, passing along the shoreline before returning to the path.

The pool opened at seven and a few of my compatriots appeared, nude as usual. They caught sight of me and sprinted over, heads bobbing. It was our duty to guard our distant cousins until the day warmed up.

Our brigade of four was enough to fend off the pool staff, and as word spread our numbers grew. We formed a perimeter up and down the path. Passersby could still walk around us, but many stayed and took photos. The hirsute man puffed his chest, playing it up for the cameras. The hairless man gleamed in the sun. And soon our friends began to awaken, their limbs coming to life, claws clutching the air as if testing it, tentative tails probing the ground before flipping bodies over onto all fours. Those already upright began to rise, slowly, up and down, again and again, increasing in speed like so many pushups. We all joined in, the moment building in intensity, until the first lizard took off down the path. And then it was off to the races. We flooded the path, dashing away from the resort. Onward we ran, the wind at our backs. It was glorious to be there, among our people, sprinting in the sun. The ocean applauded us. The palms waved goodbye.

Acknowledgments

I'm thankful: to Teresa Carmody, Hunter Choate, and Veronica Gonalez Peña for their insight into early drafts of this story; to my writing group for their consistent support and energy – Chad Anderson, Raj Reddy, Ruth Aitken, Matt Emery, and Teresa (again, without question); to Shane Hinton and Jared Silvia, two of my favorite writers, for their friendship, amorphous creative inspiration, and a shared penchant for the weird; and to Josh Dale and the Thirty West team for providing a welcome home for this book. I wrote the first draft of this story in one furious sitting while I was in the middle of reading Amparo Dávila's *The Houseguest*. That collection was certainly a catalyst and I hope this story carries some of Señora Dávila's wild-but-keen energy. A debt is also owed to philosophical works on whiteness by George Yancy and Charles W. Mills, among many others. Finally, I should acknowledge that the content of this story and the books that informed it will almost certainly be deemed unsuitable for educational use under the current authoritarian white supremacist regime in Florida. The sooner we can imagine and build a world without white supremacy (whether that includes white identity or not, I don't know) the better.

About The Author

Ryan Rivas is the author of the image/textbook *Nextdoor in Colonialtown* (Autofocus, 2022). He is the Publisher of Burrow Press, and the Coordinator of MFA Publishing at Stetson University's MFA of the Americas creative writing program. A Macondo Writers Workshop fellow, his work has appeared in *Necessary Fiction*, *The Believer*, *The Rumpus*, *Literary Hub*, *Best American Nonrequired Reading 2012*, and elsewhere.

About the Publisher

Thirty West Publishing House

Handmade Chapbooks (and more) since 2015

www.thirtywestph.com / thirtywestph@gmail.com

Review our books on Amazon & Goodreads

@thirtywestph

Fall of Fiction 2023

Bardo by Joseph Edwin Haeger
(ISBN-13: 979-8-9861105-7-8)

Late Nights at Full Moon Records by Sarah Edmonds
(ISBN-13: 979-8-9861105-9-2)

Lizard People by Ryan Rivas
(ISBN-13: 979-8-9861105-8-5)

~

Fall of Fiction 2022

Broke Witch by Jessica Bonder
(ISBN-13: 979-8-9861105-3-0)

How to Keep Time by Kevin M. Kearney
(ISBN-13: 979-8-9861105-1-6)

Tentacles Numbing by Shome Dasgupta
(ISBN-13: 979-8-9861105-2-3)